Daisy Dreamer and the World of Make-Believe

For Boop and the Bearios
—G. S.

#2

Daisy DREAMER

and the
World of Make-Believe

By Holly Anna • Illustrated by Genevieve Santos

LITTLE SIMON

New York London Toronto Sydney New Delhi

LITTLE SIMON

An imprint of Simon & Schuster Children's Publishing Division

1230 Avenue of the Americas, New York, New York 10020

First Little Simon hardcover edition April 2017

Copyright © 2017 by Simon & Schuster, Inc.

Also available in a Little Simon paperback edition.

All rights reserved, including the right of reproduction in whole or in part in any form.

LITTLE SIMON is a registered trademark of Simon & Schuster, Inc., and associated colophon is a trademark of Simon & Schuster, Inc. For information about special discounts for bulk purchases, please contact Simon & Schuster Special Sales at 1-866-506-1949 or business@simonandschuster.com. The Simon & Schuster Speakers Bureau can bring authors to your live event. For more information or to book an event contact the Simon & Schuster Speakers Bureau at 1-866-248-3049 or visit our website at www.simonspeakers.com.

Designed by Laura Roode

Manufactured in the United States of America 0217 FFG

2 4 6 8 10 9 7 5 3 1

Library of Congress Cataloging-in-Publication Data

Names: Anna, Holly. | Santos, Genevieve, illustrator.

Title: Daisy Dreamer and the world of make-believe / Holly Anna ;
illustrated by Genevieve Santos.

Description: First Little Simon paperback edition. | New York : Little Simon, 2017.

Series: Daisy Dreamer ; 2 | Summary: "Daisy Dreamer's totally true imaginary friend, Posey, invites her to explore his amazing World of Make-Believe"—Provided by publisher.

Identifiers: LCCN 2016029846 | ISBN 9781481486330 (pbk) | ISBN 9781481486347 (hc) | ISBN 9781481486354 (eBook)

Subjects: | CYAC: Imagination—Fiction. | Imaginary playmates—Fiction.

BISAC: JUVENILE FICTION / Readers / Chapter Books. | JUVENILE FICTION / Imagination & Play. | JUVENILE FICTION / Humorous Stories.

Classification: LCC PZ7.1.A568 Dc 2017 | DDC [Fic]—dc23

LC record available at https://lccn.loc.gov/2016029846

CONTENTS

CHAPTER ONE

The Magic Door

Is this really true? Is this really happening to me? Am I, Daisy Dreamer, actually going to visit an imaginary world . . . ?

"Are you ready, Daisy?" asks Posey, my very real imaginary friend.

I think hard. But only for one second, because do I want to see a world full of magical stuff? You better believe I do!

"YES!" I shout and jump, jump, jump for joy. *Obviously.* "But how do we get there?"

Now, I have been to lots of places in my life. I've been to my grandma Upsy's house, and I went to the aquarium on our first-grade field trip. I've even had a sleepover at my best friend Lily's house! But I've never been someplace imaginary.

Posey doesn't answer my question. He's too busy going through my stuff. *So how do you get to an imaginary place? I ask myself. Do you have to wear magic shoes? Or fly on a winged hippopotamus? Or take a hot-air balloon?*

Then *WHACK!* A sock hits me in the side of the head.

"OW!" I say, even though it doesn't really hurt.

Then *WHOOSH!* I duck out of the way of my hairbrush just in time.

Hey, that WOULD have hurt! I say to myself, and I shield my head with one hand.

"What do you think you're DOING?!" I shout as things continue to fly across my room. Posey is pulling stuff out of my drawers. There goes a doll . . . and a shoe . . . and a . . .

"What's this?" Posey asks. He's holding up a pair of my *underwear!*

"Hey, put those DOWN!" I shout. "That is so embarrassing!" *Obviously.*

Then I stomp toward Posey. "That's enough!" I say. "I'm drawing the line!"

Posey stops and looks up. "No, I'm drawing the line," he replies. "But I need something to draw it with!"

"Huh?" I say. "What are you talking about?"

"I'm looking for a mark maker," Posey says, digging through my dresser drawers. "We need to draw a magic mark to get to the World of Make-Believe, but I can't find anything to draw with!"

"You mean like a marker or a pen?" I ask.

"Yes," he says. "One of those things that squeaks when you draw things!"

"Like this?" I pull a marker out of my desk drawer. It's the only place in my room he hasn't completely messed up yet.

"Perfect!" Posey says as I hand it

to him. He pops off the top and goes straight for my wall.

"Whoa, back up, imaginary friend!" I shout—and just in time. Posey is about to *draw* on my *wall*! "You can't do that. I'll get in *so* much trouble!"

Posey folds his arms and taps one foot. "Look, if you *really* want to go to the World of Make-Believe, then we're going to need a *door. Obviously.*"

I feel my cheeks grow hot. Is it my imagination, or did Posey just sound like *me*?

"Okay," I say. "Then at least use *this* pen. It's totally erasable." I hand him a purple pen.

Then Posey draws a door on my wall and tosses the pen behind him onto the floor. "Are you ready now?" he asks.

"Hmm, not dressed like this!" I say. "The World of Make-Believe deserves a totally new outfit because it's a totally new place!"

Then I hurry-rush to the bathroom wondering what could be behind Posey's drawn door.

☆ CHAPTER TWO ☆

The World of Make-Believe

Now I am *so* ready!

Or, at least, I think I'm ready. Come to think of it, I'm a little worried. I gnaw the back of my thumb.

"It—it is almost dinnertime, you know," I say, stammering. "Won't my mom and dad worry if I suddenly disappear?" I swallow hard. "Maybe we shouldn't go."

Posey waves me off. "Not to worry!" he says. "No one will even know you're gone. Time in the World of Make-Believe is imaginary, so it takes no real time at all. Plus, when someone wants you back, all they have to do is call your name."

It sounds safe enough, so I stick both thumbs up. "In that case . . . RACE YOU TO THE DOOR!"

Posey runs, but I grab hold of the knob first. One turn, and *SWOOSH!* My bedroom is *gone!*

Instead, we're standing on a RAINBOW ROAD! It's bouncy, like a

trampoline. Now I *know* we're in the World of Make-Believe.

"Come on!" says Posey. "Let me show you around!"

He grabs my hand, and . . . *Boing!*

Boing! We begin to bounce down the road. By golly, we're bouncing over the rainbow! And everything looks different here. The grass is blue! The sky is yellow! And the flowers are *lollipops.*

I stop and pick one. It's blue raspberry! I lick it and look up to the sky. Fluffy multicolored clouds float by like cotton candy. They are shaped like animals: lions, bears, horses, and dogs!

Then I notice a pearl-colored unicorn cloud. It's peeking out from behind an elephant cloud. The unicorn hides when I look at it.

Hey, I think that unicorn cloud is spying on me!

☆ CHAPTER THREE ☆

Andever

"It *is* spying on me!" I shout, pointing to the sky.

Posey looks up and smiles. "Oh, that's a Cloud Critter," he says. "They're animals formed by clouds."

Posey whistles as the cloud unicorn begins to drift toward us. "I think she may want something. Cloud Critters rarely come down from the sky."

I watch the pearly unicorn float to the ground. She gets smaller and smaller the closer she comes! When she lands, we're basically the same size. Then the unicorn looks me over and snorts like a horse.

"Where did *you* come from?" she asks me in a very sassy voice. If Upsy were here, she would say that this Cloud Critter has "attitude."

"Me?" I say, pointing to myself. "I came from the real world." *Obviously.* I'm a little surprised to be talking to a cloud unicorn.

The unicorn shakes her misty mane and takes a step back. "I've heard of

the Real World," she says. "But I never knew it really existed."

Then she stares at me like I'm something magical. And I stare back because she *is* something magical. Then she nudges my hair, so I touch her shimmering coat. It feels cool and airy, just like a cloud. She nickers softly.

Posey clears his throat to get our attention. "Andever, this is my imaginary friend, Daisy," he says. "Daisy, this is Andever."

Whoa, I think to myself. *Posey has it all backward.* I stop and correct

him. "*I'm* not your imaginary friend," I say firmly. "You are *my* imaginary friend."

Posey laughs. "Well, that might be true in *your* world, but in *my* world, I'm the normal one."

I scrunch up my face and think about it. Posey may have a point there. Could I really be the imaginary friend? That's weird, but I like it.

"It's nice to meet you," I finally say.

Andever gives me a thoughtful head nod.

"So, what brings you down from the sky, Andever?" Posey asks. "Is everything all right?"

Andever shakes her wispy mane. "No," she says sadly. "I've lost something very dear to me."

Posey and I look at each other.

"What can it be?" I ask curiously.

Andever shuffles her hoof and sighs heavily. "I've lost my . . . my . . . my melody!" she says, beginning to weep.

Then I notice something unusual. Cloud Critters cry raindrops.

"Is your melody like a song?" I ask.

"Yes, but it's more than a song,"

Andever says. "My melody helps make me *me*. All Cloud Critters have their own special melody."

I look at Posey. He shrugs. We have no idea what Andever is talking about.

"Can you tell us what it looks like?" I ask, hoping to find a clue.

"I keep it in my locket most of the time," says Andever. "But when I take it out, my melody shimmers and glows in a great ball of music and light."

Magnificent, I think. Then I look at her golden locket. It's around her neck, and guess what? It's unlatched.

"My melody must have fallen out while I was flying!" Andever cries.

She's right—the locket is empty. Then I look at Posey, and I can tell he's thinking what I'm thinking.

We have to help Andever find her melody . . . whatever it turns out to actually be!

☆ CHAPTER FOUR ☆

The Game Plan

"It's simple!" Posey says. "All we have to do is retrace your flight today."

Andever looks away. "But how?" she says helplessly. "I've been all over the WOM today."

This makes me raise an eyebrow. "The WOM?" I question.

"*The World of Make-Believe!*" they both say at the same time.

I blush a little. *"Obviously,"* I say. "But Posey's right—retracing your flight is the best way to find your melody."

"Oh no!" Andever says as she runs and hides behind a pink gumdrop hedge. Her horn pokes up from behind a bush.

Posey and I rush to Andever's not-very-good hiding spot.

"Why are you hiding?" Posey asks. "Are you afraid of something?"

Andever makes the bush quiver. "Yes, I'm afraid of the M-M-M-M-Moonsturs!" she cries. "You see, I flew over Moonstur Hollow today."

Then I put my hands on my hips and look at Posey. "What the boo-hilly are Moonsturs?"

"Moonsturs are a kid's worst fears—come to life," Posey says with a frown. "They can be the thing that lives under your bed or the thing that lurks in your closet or that dreadful thing that waits in the basement for no good reason at all except to scare people."

Hmm . . . I'm pretty sure there's a Moonstur in our linen closet.

Posey continues. "I've seen them before. They are shaggy, slobbery, and all-around scary."

Andever nods wildly. She's shaking into little puffs of nervous clouds.

Wow, they seem scared. Here's the problem. I can't figure out what everybody is so afraid of because Moonsturs don't sound scary to me at all. They sound cool! So I pump my fists and shout. "What are we waiting for? Let's go to Moonstur Hollow!"

CHAPTER FIVE

Moonstur Hollow

Posey and Andever stare at me with their mouths hanging open.

"What?" I say innocently. "It'll be an adventure. Besides, you have to face your fears! That's what my grandma Upsy always says, and she's *really* smart."

So Posey leads the way to Moonstur Hollow, and let me tell you, it is not on the Rainbow Road. Moonstur Hollow is as dark as a gray day in November. And it looks like a spooky bedroom. I mean, it has actual rickety children's beds with moth-eaten dust ruffles, weather-beaten rocking chairs, and

dressers sticking out of the ground like boats in the ocean. There are even random doorways in the dirt with stairs that lead underground.

"I GET IT!" I cry out loud. "This must be where the Moonsturs practice their hiding and scaring skills. Then, when they go to a *real* kid's bedroom, they'll know just what to do."

Posey cups his hand over my mouth. *Was I too loud?* I wonder. Then we hear a deep, rumbly voice.

"You called?" the voice growls.

I notice something with shaggy green fur lurking not too far from us. It has one too many toes; big, droopy ears; thick, bushy eyebrows; a large pink nose; and a mouthful of pointy yellow teeth. I'm pretty sure  it's a Moonstur. And it's *absolutely* adorable in the weirdest way!

"Hi there!" I say.

The Moonstur looks over both of his shoulders as if I'm talking to somebody else. Then he looks back at me. "Why you no run and hide?" he says. He talks with a *grrr* in his voice. Then he jerks a thumb at Andever and Posey, who are hiding behind a tree. "Those two run and hide. They smart."

I shake my head. "They just don't see how wonderful you are."

"WHAT?!" he shouts and waves his arms in the air. "Me NOT wonderful!!! Me GRACKAN. Everyone say me SCARY. You RUN!"

Aw, this Moonstur needs a great big hug, but I offer him my hand instead. "Nice to meet you, Grackan the Wonderful!" I say, shaking his furry green hand. *He's a snuggle bug, I think, except for maybe all those pointy teeth.*

"Grackan da Won-dur-fool?" he repeats. I can tell he likes it, but then

he gets all gruff again. "So, what you want?"

I look over at Andever. "That Cloud Critter has lost her melody. Have you seen it?"

"Is it bright, shiny, NOISY?" asks Grackan, and I give him a nod.

A big toothy smile spreads across his furry face. "Me help." Andever lets out a hopeful cry, but Grackan holds up a claw.

"FIRST we play hide-and-shriek!" he says. "THEN me help."

I step up and answer for everyone. "Let's play!"

Grackan is "it" first. He counts, and we scatter. Not to brag, but I am a master hider. I dive under the covers of one of the messy, unmade beds.

I fluff the quilt to make it look like
nobody is there. Posey hides
in a closet. *Bad idea.*
Andever hides behind
a bush. *Worse idea.*
They both get
caught, *obviously,*
and Grackan gives
them a good scare.

I know because I hear them shriek.

Then we all take turns being "it." Grackan is a master hider too. When he disguises himself as a furry footstool, no one finds him!

"ME win!" Grackan says triumphantly. "Now me tell you what me know."

We gather round and listen eagerly.

"Your melody disturbing Pretty Pixies," he says. Then he turns to me. "You go see. You find. You good at hide, which mean you good at find."

Now I think that is a Moonstur compliment! So off we go to the Land of the Pretty Pixies.

CHAPTER SIX

Land of the Pretty Pixies

"Pretty Pixies are very hard to spot," Posey says as we walk along a woodland path.

I'm not sure what I'm looking for, but I can see trees, ferns, flowers, wild berries, and clusters of polka-dot mushrooms. I can also hear the sound of a bubbling brook nearby. These woods are perfect—no fallen trees or dead leaves, or any trace of icky, itchy poison ivy.

"Are we near the Land of the Pretty Pixies?" I ask.

"Very near," Posey says. "In fact, we may be standing in the Land of the Pretty Pixies right now—so watch your step!"

"Wow, they must be tiny!" Andever exclaims.

"A Pretty Pixie village can fit inside a burgabane box," Posey tells us.

"Okay." I pause. "Are you going to tell me what a burgabane is?"

"It's food made with cheese and tomato sauce on round bread," says Posey. "You've probably never heard of it."

"You mean pizza?" I ask. "*Obviously,* I know pizza. It's delicious! Wait, the entire village can fit in a burgabane box?"

That is very small! I think. Then I quickly check the bottom of my shoe to make sure I haven't stepped on a Pretty Pixie. Andever checks under her hooves too.

"Have you ever heard of pixie dust?" Posey asks.

I put a hand on my hip. *"Obviously,"* I say. "Who hasn't?"

Posey rolls his eyes. "Well, Pretty Pixies *are* pixie dust! And have you ever noticed dust sparkling in a beam of light?"

Andever and I both nod.

"Those are Pretty Pixies in their Pretty Pixie Dust form! It's how they sneak around."

"Wow, wow, triple wow," I say. "I never knew *that* before!"

Note to self: Look more closely at sparkling dust beams from now on.

Then I walk right into a swarm of gnats. Ugh! I brush them away, but they come right back. I wave my hands like crazy to shoo them away. And then I take a closer look and gasp.

"Oh no! These are *not* gnats!" I cry. "It's Pretty Pixie dust!"

The Pretty Pixie dust swoops down toward a tiny pixie village. Then the dust forms into tiny pixies in flower-petal clothes!

Their town has itsy-bitsy houses

with pinecone scales for shingles. There are eensy-weensy rustic twig chairs and tables. I see winding pebble paths and elven bridges that lead to wee playgrounds with leaf hammocks and acorn swings. It's an itty-bitty paradise!

I hold out the palm of my hand, and one of the little pixies lands on it. Her voice sounds like tiny tinkling bells. I lift my palm closer to my ear to hear her speak.

"My name is Twee," she says. "The Pretty Pixies wish to know if you mean us any harm."

I answer softly so as not to hurt her ears. "I'm Daisy," I whisper. "And we mean you no harm at all. We're only looking for my friend's lost melody."

"Oh!" Twee twitters. "Is the melody very loud and musical?"

I nod. "And bright and shiny."

"Your friend's melody is beautiful," says Twee. "But it was too loud and bright for tiny sprites like us. We had the Golly Ghosts take it away."

"The who?" I ask too loudly, and Twee flits away from my hand.

Posey knows exactly who she is talk-ing about. "Uh-oh," he says. "The Golly Ghosts are troublemakers. They're also very fond of treasure."

Andever shakes her mane with con-cern. "Oh dear. My melody is doomed! I could turn into a storm cloud with-out my melody."

I shake my finger at Andever.

"We're not going to give up now," I say firmly. "We are going to see the Golly Ghosts. I have handled a few trouble-makers in my world, you know."

And, without another word, we're on our way . . . careful not to step on the itty-bitty village below.

Chapter Seven

The Golly Ghost Town

Fog billows through the Golly Ghost town. Everything here has a ghostly form, from the see-through houses and stores to the ghostly people. Even the trees are strung with ghostly gray moss, like long, shaggy grandpa beards.

"Wooooooooooooooooooooooooooo!" (Did I mention that there is lot of moaning here too?)

"Quit tapping my shoulder," Posey whispers.

"I didn't do that," I whisper back.

Then something taps Posey again. He looks all around. Then something else trips Andever and she stumbles to the ground. Her cloudy form puffs apart and re-forms itself. We hear a chorus of creepy laughter.

Then *OW!* Somebody yanks my pigtails. I spin around to see who did it, but no one is there. Okay, now I'm *mad*.

"*Enough!*" I say in my best serious-mom voice. "Show yourselves!"

And whoa! It works! Nobody messes with a serious-mom voice. *Obviously.*

Three Golly Ghosts appear right in front of us. How can I make these tricksters stop being tricky? Hmm . . . Then I think of a word my mom

taught me when I was complaining about Gabby, the meanest girl in my whole school. "Diplomacy."

I imagine the letters written in my journal: D-I-P-L-O-M-A-C-Y. It means to be fair, thoughtful, and clever when dealing with others. I can be diplomatic! So I turn to the ghosts.

"Oh, what *smart* Gollies!" I say, complimenting them. "You did an expert job sneaking up on us!" This is being diplomatic—and very clever. *Obviously.* I go on. "We could sure use some help from gifted ghosts like yourselves!"

"We know-o-o-o!" they wail.

I'm pretty sure my diplomacy is working, so I keep going. "This is my friend Andever. She lost her melody, and we need your help to find it."

"We'll never tehhh-ell!" They moan and dance around us. This whole moaning thing is getting old, but at least it proves they know something about the lost melody.

Then I feel something on my back.

I spin around. Posey is holding a sign that says PRANK ME.

"This was stuck to your back," Posey says, shredding the sign. "But I stopped those tricky Golly Ghosts!"

I hold my hand up in front of Posey. "Thanks for standing up for me," I say.

Posey slaps me five. "That's what friends do!"

Then the Golly Ghosts begin to slap each other five too.

"Are you making fun of us again?" Posey asks them.

"Not at all," they say in totally normal-sounding, nonghostly voices. "We like it when friends stick up for each other. And now we'll stick up for you, too. Plus, we'll tell you about the lost melody."

Andever neighs her approval. "So where is it?"

"We gave it to Red Fox," the first Golly says.

"He said it belonged to him," says the second ghost. "He even sang to it."

"Oh, what a sneaky beast!" cries Andever. "He wanted that melody all for himself!"

Then I shake my head at those Golly Ghosts and tell them, "Guess what? You got outfoxed . . . by a fox! Now, where can we find that rascal?"

Posey answers me with a smile. "Looks like you get to meet the Forest Friends, Daisy Dreamer."

Chapter Eight

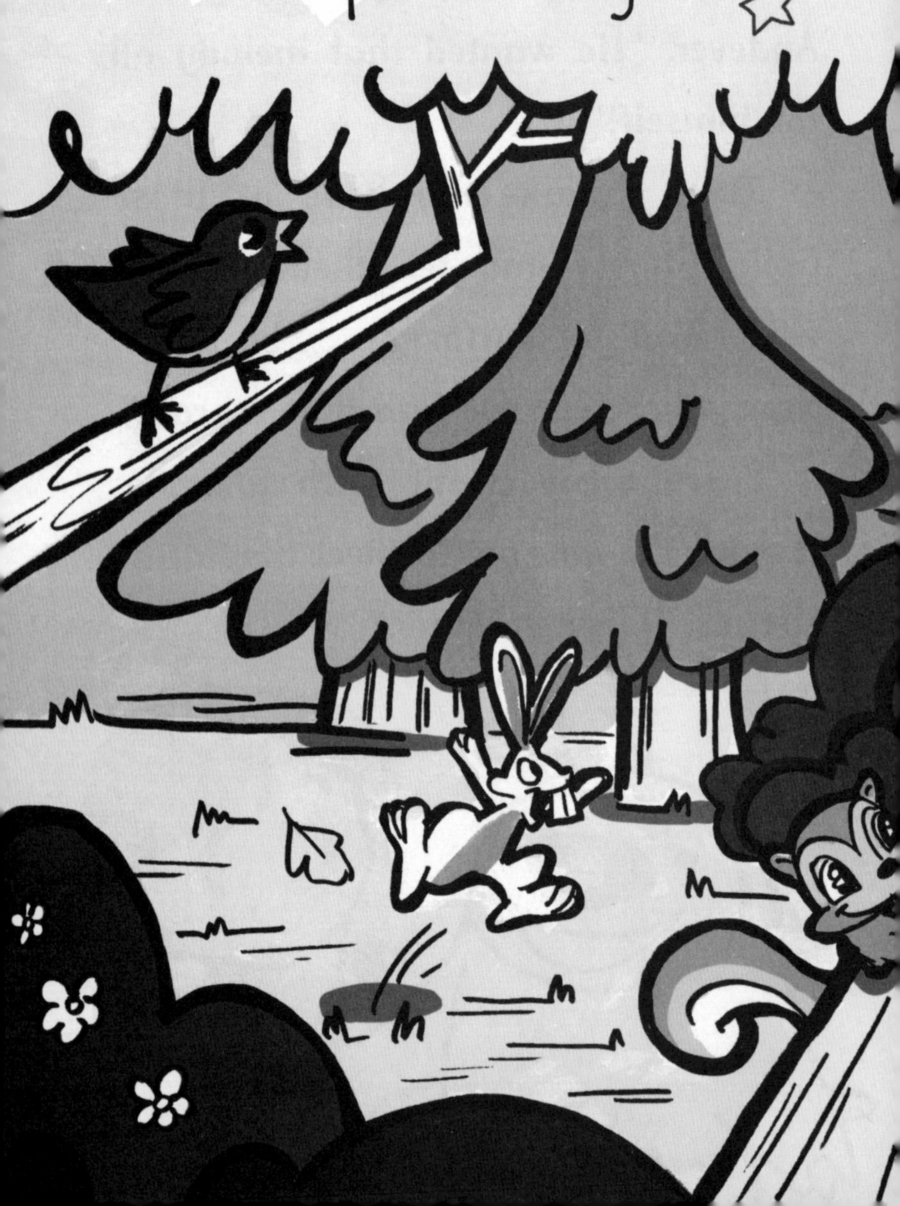

Forest Friends

Forest Friends live in the Friendly Forest. Duh. But it's not an ordinary forest. Not. At. All.

It feels like stepping into a cartoon. That's because I *did*. A cartoon bunny hops across the trail. A comic-book squirrel twitches its tail while climbing up the side of a tree drawing. There are even cartoon birds singing in the branches above us, but they're not tweedle-deeting—they are singing *actual words!*

A pretty yellow canary flutters down and perches on my finger. "You look lost," she sings.

"Do you know where Red Fox lives?" I ask.

"He lives in the hollow tree," she sings. "Follow me!"

The cheery canary leads us to an arched door in a tree trunk.

Posey raps the door knocker. *Tap! Tap! Tap!*

Red Fox cracks it open and squints at us suspiciously.

"We are missing a melody," says Posey.

"A melody, you say?" He strokes the fur on his chin. "Who's heard of such a thing?" Then he slams the door shut.

Such a silly fox! I think. *There's no way we'll give up THAT easily.*

So we knock again and he answers.

"It's shiny and bright and glowy and showy," I tell him.

"Shiny and bright, you say?" he repeats. "Glowy and showy?" He lets out a great big laugh. Then he goes right back to a straight face. "I have no idea what you're talking about," he says sternly and slams the door again.

"WAIT!" I shout. "We heard you were the cleverest Forest Friend."

The fox peeks out again and sighs. "*Obviously*," he says, stealing *my* word.

But I keep cool. "After all, don't you have the sharpest see-in-the-dark eyes, the keenest all-hearing ears, and the niftiest nose in all the World of Make-Believe?"

Red Fox opens the door wider. "That would be *me*!" he says proudly.

I take a step closer. "Surely someone as clever as you would be the first
to know of a lost melody! Unless, of
course, someone else already beat you
to it. . . ."

Red Fox jabs his thumb at his chest.
"I saw it *first!*"

Posey hops in front of me. "So you
have seen it!"

Red Fox realizes he's given himself away. "Well, I—I might've seen a
melody," he stammers. "But I can't be
certain."

Andever paws the ground uneasily
with her hoof. "Oh, please! You must

give my melody back. It's my joy, my sparkle, my song!"

Red Fox slumps his shoulders and comes all the way out of his tree house. "Oh, very well. How can I steal some-one's joy? You can find your melody if you can solve this riddle."

Apparently, foxes love riddles, so we gather round as he begins. "Silent and still, gazing upward all day, it's a place where fish love to play. Frogs on lily pads asleep and awake. At night the moon reflects on the . . ."

"MARSHMALLOW!" shout Andever and Posey.

I shake my head. No, no, *no*! "It's *not* a marshmallow, you sillies! It's a *lake*! At night the moon reflects on the *lake*!"

And then I realize something. . . . I totally know what Andever's melody really is, and I know where to find it!

Chapter Nine

Star Bright Lake

"Posey, where's the nearest lake?" I ask.

He points down the forest path. "Star Bright Lake is over there. Why?"

Without answering, I take off down the trail. Posey and Andever scramble after me. It's getting dark outside, and the moon is rising in the night sky. We come to a clearing, and there's the lake. The moon and stars reflect on

the water like shiny gems. We walk to
the shore and look into the lake.

"Where's my melody?" asks Andever.

I gaze at the water. "Hmm, it's shiny
and bright. And glowy and showy."

"Like a star," says Posey, admiring
the reflection in the lake.

"Andever," I say, "Your melody is
a *star*!"

The Cloud Critter neighs happily,

but then she stops. "Wait. There are so many stars reflected here. Which one is *mine*?"

Posey skips a stone, and the surface of the lake ripples. "Your melody is part of your song. Maybe if you sing your song, your melody will answer."

Andever steps to the water's edge.

Her golden locket glints in the moon-light. "But without my melody, I'll sing off-key!"

I walk over and stroke Andever's wispy mane. "It doesn't matter if you sing off-key. I'd bet your melody will know you because it's yours and nobody else's. When it comes back, you will be in harmony again!"

Andever begins to sing softly. Her voice grows stronger with each note she sings. Then one star on the lake begins to shimmer and glow. It's brighter than all the others.

Whoosh!

All at once a streak of light shoots out of the lake and right into Andever's locket. Her song and her melody become a beautiful chorus.

"There you are, Forever!" Andever cries, greeting her lost melody.

Posey dances along to the melody.
"Forever *And*-ever!" he cries. "You two
really *do* belong together!"

The Cloud Critter admires her glow-
ing locket. "And you will be my friends
forever and ever too."

Posey and I hug Andever for a long time. Then we watch her fly into the starry night, and we listen to her beautiful song. But I also hear something else.

"Daiiiiiissyyy!" the wind whispers. "Daiiiiiissyyy!"

Somebody is calling my name.

☆ CHAPTER Ten ☆

Spiraling

Then *SWOOSH!* Something strange happens. The WOM begins to spin. I grab hold of Posey, and we begin to swirl round and round.

"WHAT'S HAPPENING?" I yell into the whistling wind.

Posey squeezes my hand. "Don't worry. Just hold on, and enjoy the ride!"

So I squeeze my eyes shut and pretend to enjoy spiraling through space. I can still hear someone calling my name in the distance. *Am I dreaming?* I wonder. Soon the wind and the spinning slow down. Then everything becomes still. And quiet.

I open my eyes, and I'm back in my bedroom!

"Calling Daisy Dreamer! Earth to Daisy Dreamer! Suppertime!" It's my dad.

But where's Posey? I jump to my feet and check my closet. Nothing. I lie

on my stomach to look under my bed.
Nothing. Posey's gone! I look across
the room. Even the door Posey drew
on my wall is gone!

I blink and sit down. Did I imagine
the *whole thing*?

My cat, Sir Pounce, crawls onto my lap and paws at a piece of paper sticking out of my pocket. I pull it out. It's a note that reads:

Dear Daisy,

Thank you for visiting my world. Next time I'll introduce you to the Sparkle Fairies and the Imaginaries. Did you know I'm an Imaginary? I can't wait for our next ADVENTURE.

love, POSEY

Hi!

I look into Sir Pounce's green eyes.

"So it *was* all true! I *knew* it!"

I get up, and Sir Pounce runs away.

Then I pull the special journal Upsy

gave me out from under my bed. I'm going to write down *everything* that happened in here.

But first I'm going to eat dinner because it's been a *big* day. And I am *so* hungry.

Obviously.

Check out Daisy Dreamer's next adventure!

Scritch-scratch!

Scritch-scratch!

I crawl through the starry-smooth tunnel to the Hideout—our secret meeting place under the slide at school. Jasmine and Lily scuff along behind me. Then we sit crisscross applesauce

Excerpt from *Sparkle Fairies and the Imaginaries*

on the ground. I swish pebbles out from under me.

"The meeting of the Secret Journal Club is now called to order!" I say as I open my secret journal. It was a gift from my grandmother Upsy.

"What's on the agenda?" Lily asks, tossing her long dark hair over one shoulder.

I lean closer to my friends. "You'll never believe it," I begin.

Their eyes widen. "What?" they both say at the same time.

I check the tunnel to make sure no one's there.

Excerpt from *Sparkle Fairies and the Imaginaries*

"Remember my imaginary friend, Posey?" I ask.

Their heads bob up and down. Of course they remember Posey. It's not every day that an imaginary friend appears out of thin air right in front of you.

"Well, he drew a *magic* door on my bedroom wall and took me to the WOM!" I say, sounding out each let-ter. *Double-U. Oh. Em.*

Lily and Jasmine make funny faces, because they have no idea about the WOM.

Excerpt from *Sparkle Fairies and the Imaginaries*